All Join In

D0928513

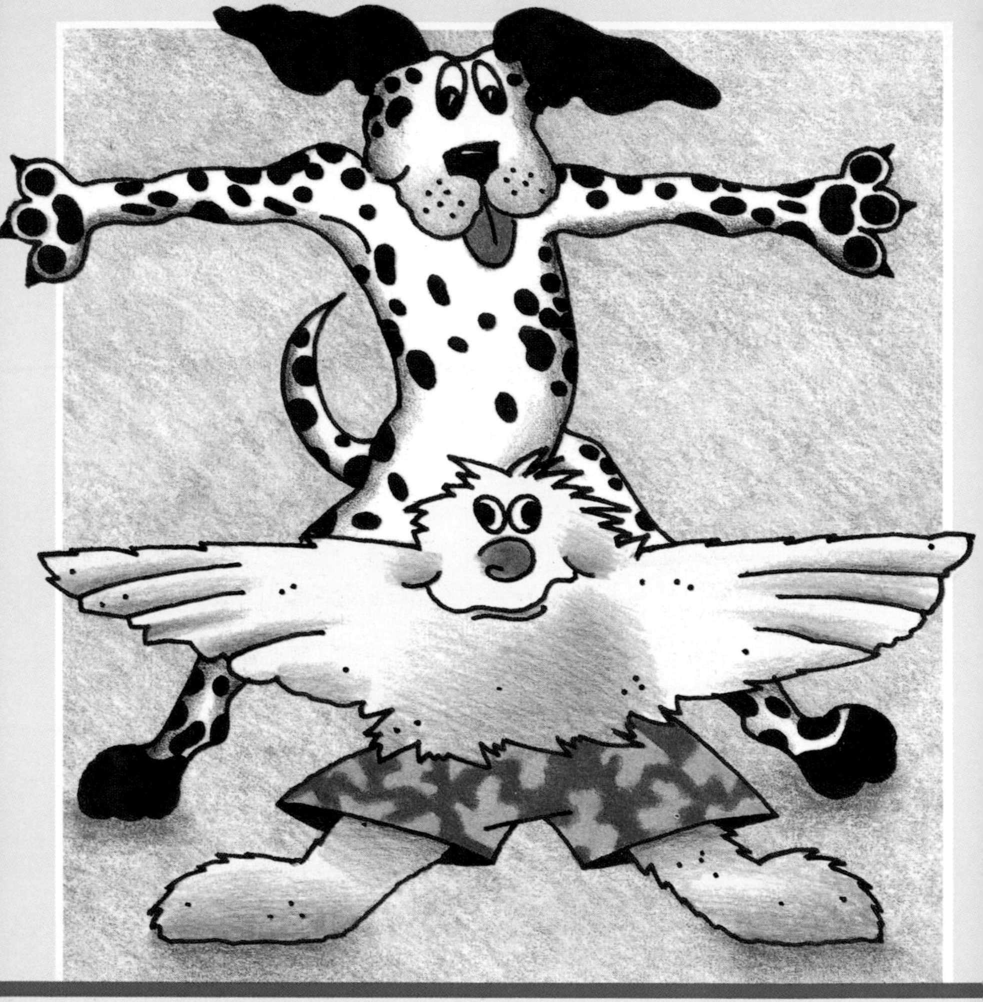

As wide as a gate.

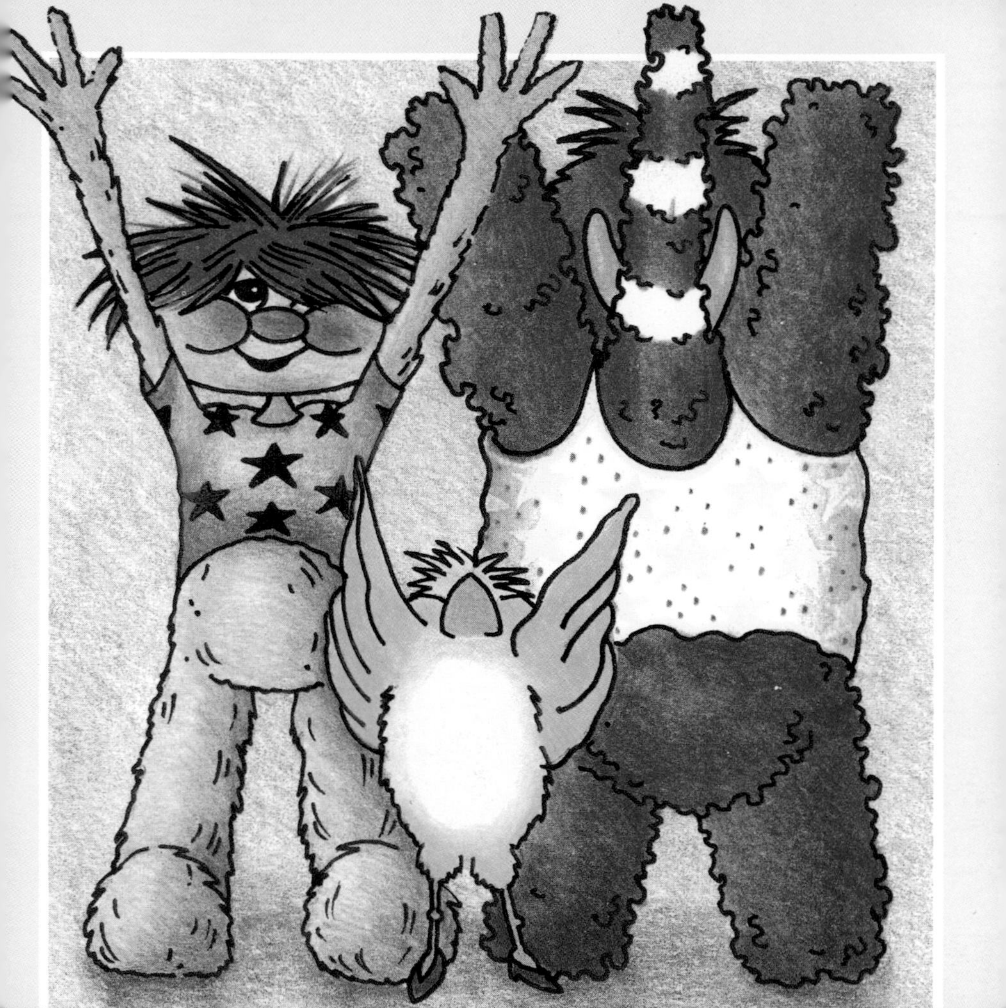

As tall as a house.

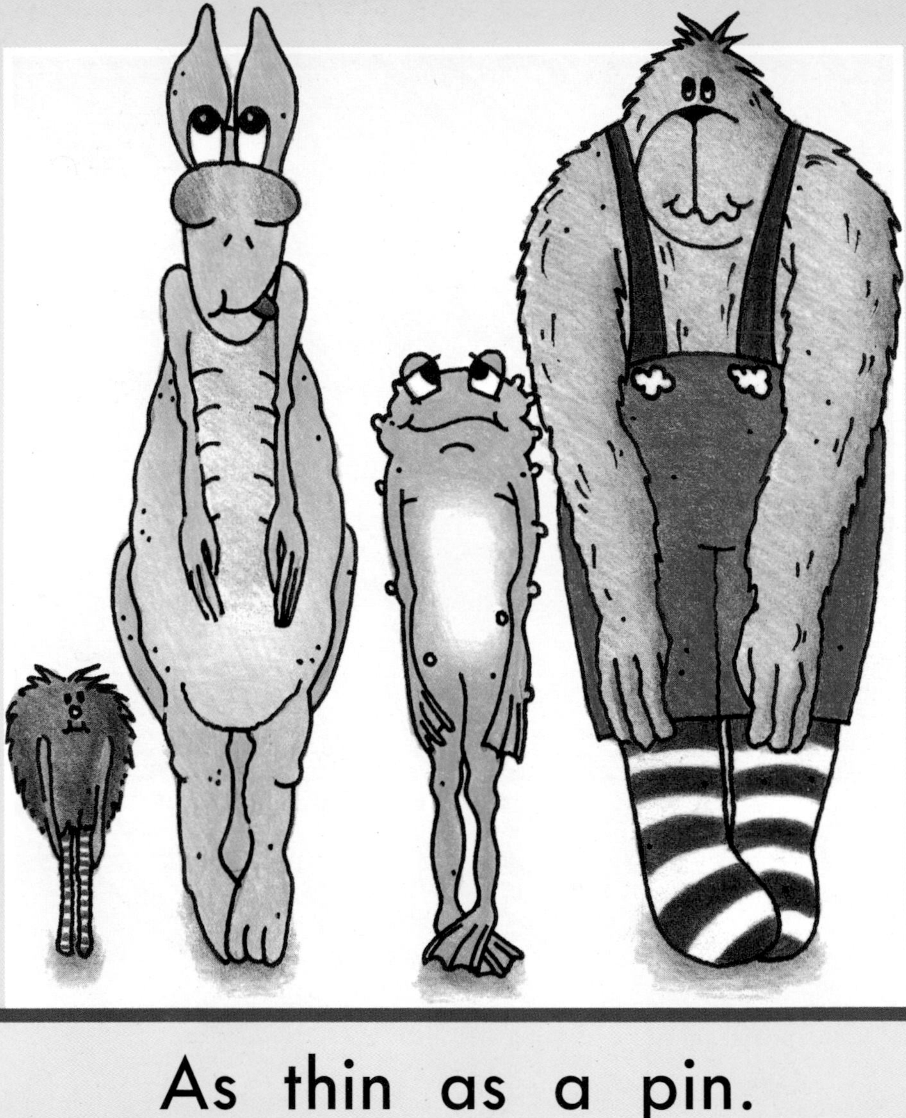

As thin as a pin.

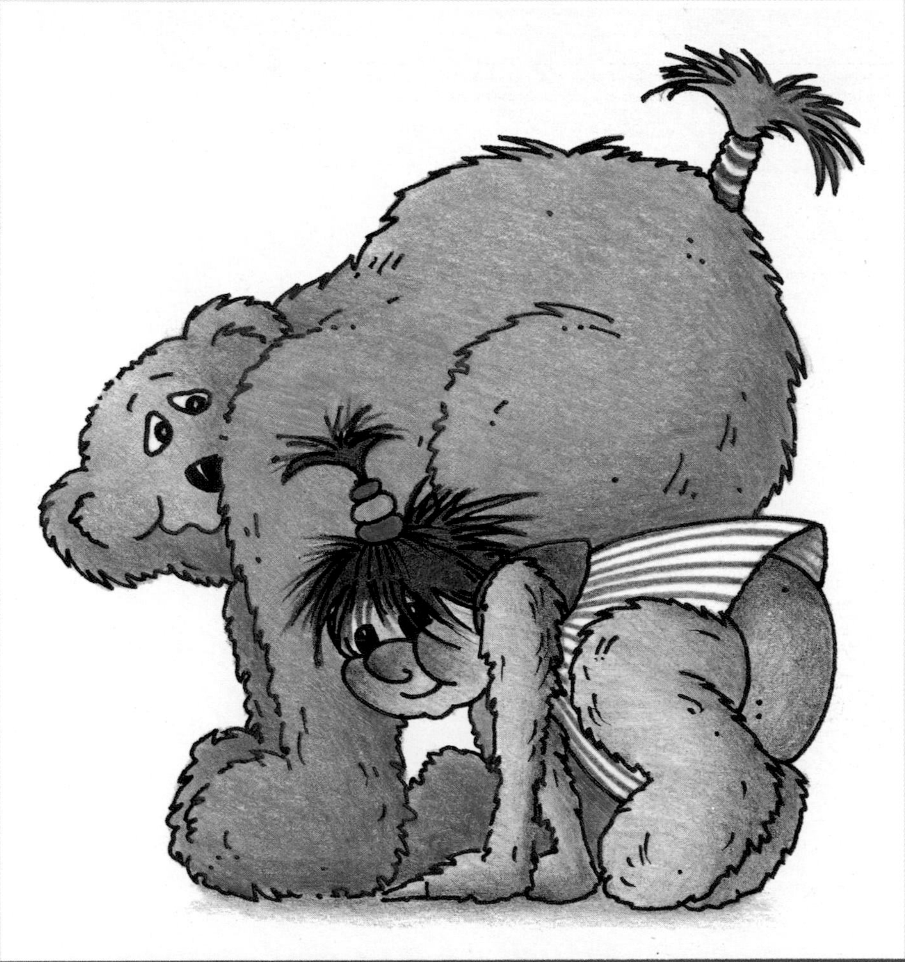

As small as a mouse.

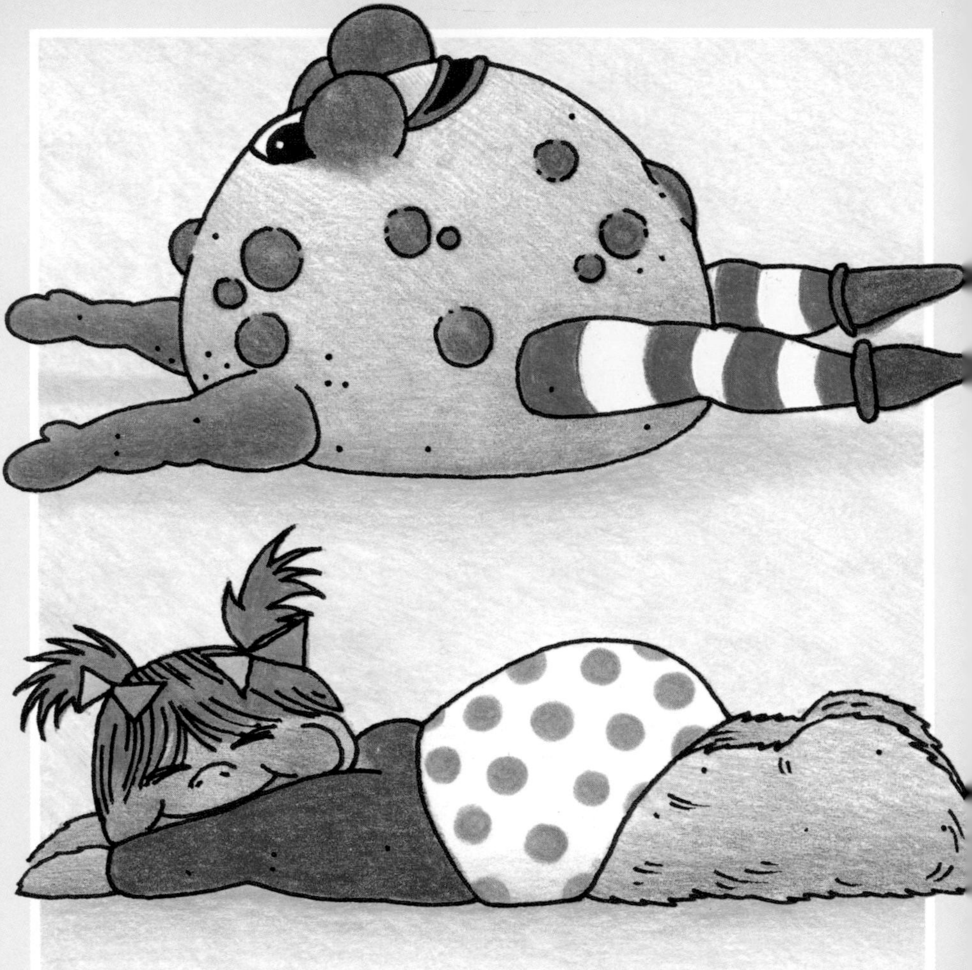

As long as a log.

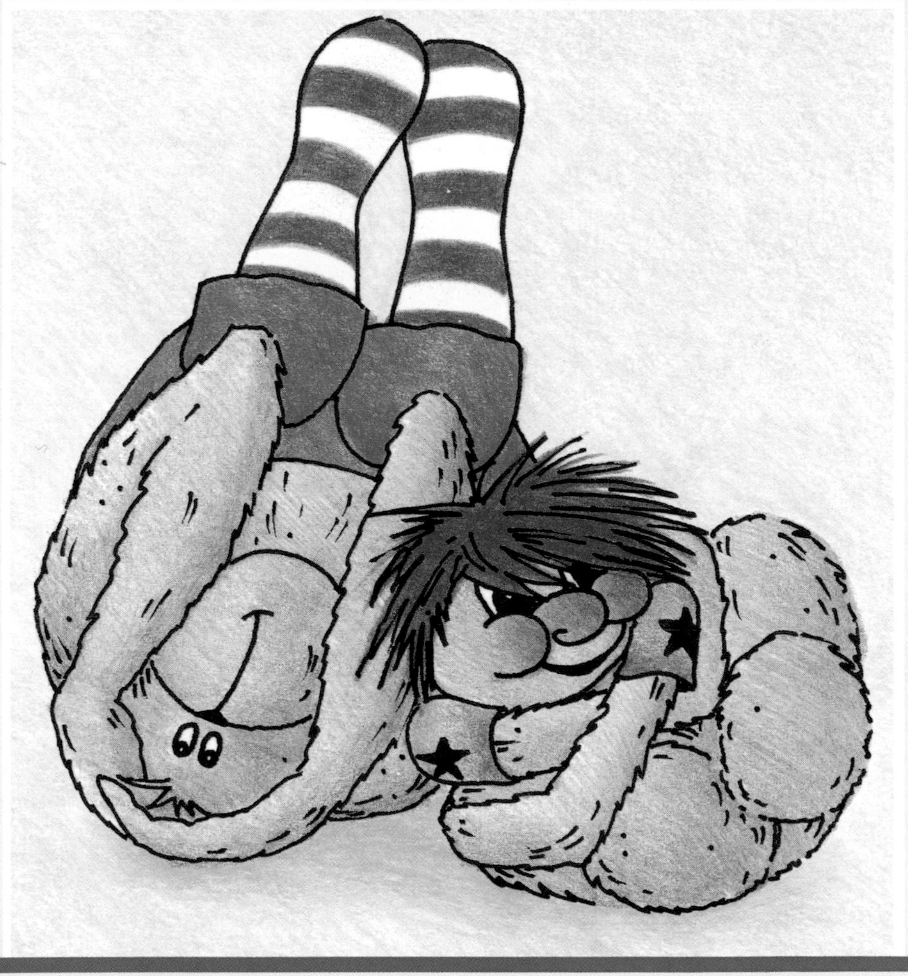

As round as a ball.

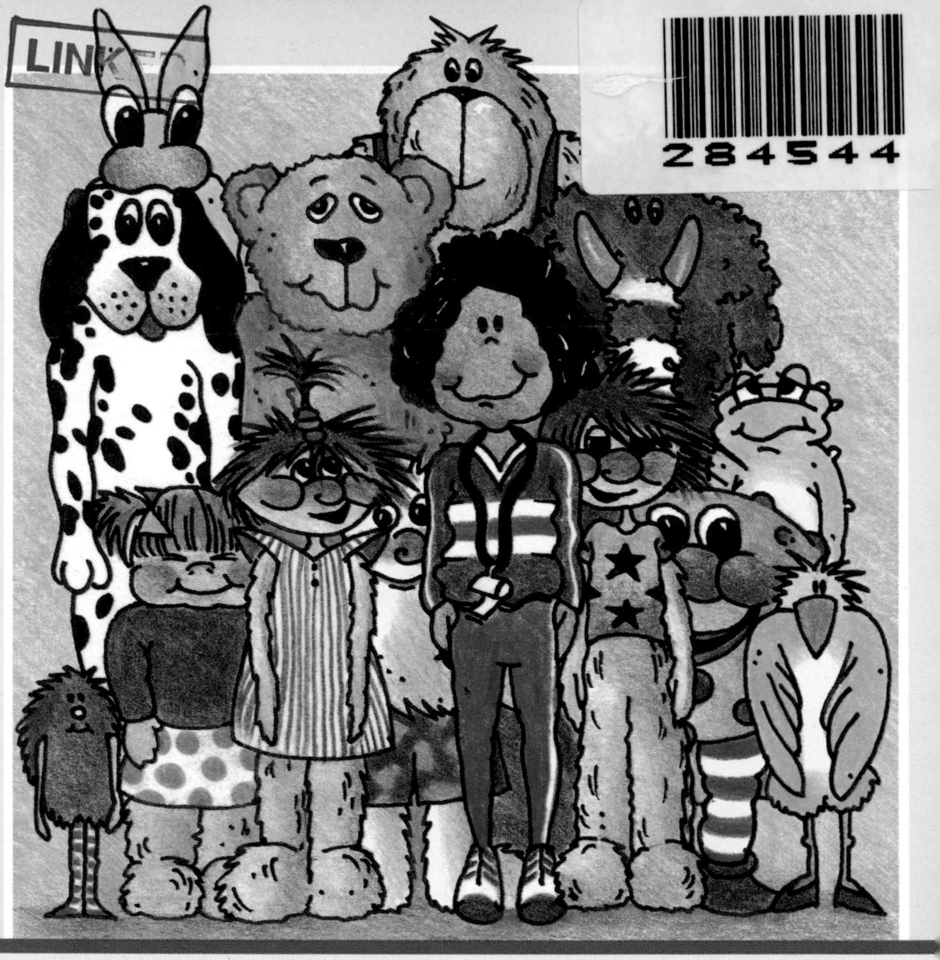

Now stand up straight,
as that is all.